THE·LAND·OF
NOD

THE
FLOATING
ISLES

THE
BLACK
MOUNTAIN

SNOWY
VILLAGE

ENCHANTED
VALLEY

CREEPY
CASTLE

GLOOMY
DEN

GLITTER
BAY

BOULDER
GORGE

N

W   E

S

THE
ANCIENT FOREST

OUTER
SPACE

EMERALD GLEN

GIANTS' TOWN

DEADLY
CREEK

RICKETY
BRIDGE

THE
STINKY
SWAMPS

GOLDEN
COVE

To Lara, Sophie and Órla
R.F.

LADYBIRD BOOKS
UK | USA | Canada | Ireland | Australia | India | New Zealand | South Africa
Ladybird Books is part of the Penguin Random House group of companies
whose addresses can be found at global.penguinrandomhouse.com.
www.penguin.co.uk   www.puffin.co.uk   www.ladybird.co.uk

Penguin
Random House
UK

First published 2023
001
Written by Rhiannon Fielding. Text copyright © Ladybird Books Ltd, 2023
Illustrations copyright © Chris Chatterton, 2023
The moral right of the illustrator has been asserted
TEN MINUTES TO™ and TEN MINUTES TO BED™ are trademarks of
Ladybird Books Ltd. All Rights Reserved.

Printed in China

The authorized representative in the EEA is Penguin Random House Ireland,
Morrison Chambers, 32 Nassau Street, Dublin D02 YH68

A CIP catalogue record for this book is available from the British Library
ISBN: 978–0–241–54563–8
All correspondence to:
Ladybird Books, Penguin Random House Children's
One Embassy Gardens, 8 Viaduct Gardens London SW11 7BW

TEN
MINUTES
TO BED

Little
Dinosaur's
Big Race

Rhiannon Fielding · Chris Chatterton

Down in the jungle on Midsummer's Eve,
there's a scene going on that you wouldn't believe!
For this time each year – as is dino tradition –
the dinosaurs all have a big competition!

In a warm, sunny spot draped with long hanging vines,
the dinosaurs queued up in jostling lines.
Ten minutes to bed! Time to start the first test –

but one dinosaur
stood apart from the rest.

"Where are his teammates?" the dinosaurs asked.

"Oh, Rumble!" they murmured.

"He'll surely come last!"

Nine minutes! A horn blared;

dust rose from the ground

as they charged to the mountain
to start the first round.

The first of the tasks was a flying routine!
In the sky, swooping pterosaurs soon could be seen.

Would his plan really work?
Just eight minutes to bed . . .

but what was
that shape, high above
Rumble's head?

A small spark of red that grew quicker and quicker –
Rumble smiled as he spotted his first teammate, Flicker!
Seven minutes to bed: time to start the next test,

for the dinos agreed –
Flicker's show
was the best!

Not far from the mountain stood thousands of trees,
and marshmallow clouds drifted by on the breeze.
Six minutes to bed: there was no time for sleeping . . .

everywhere, dinos were
jumping and **leaping!**

Dinosaurs tiny

and dinosaurs tall –

but somebody jumped
and leapt higher than all!

Five minutes: four hooves, and a glittery horn . . .

of course, it was **Twinkle**,
the small unicorn!

Together, they **raced** to a **maze** made of flowers,

whose blossoms stretched upwards like **colourful towers**.

Four minutes: when suddenly, something grew bright . . .

a fairy trail, glowing
with warm golden light.

As **Poppy** flew closer and reached her friend Rumble,
from somewhere ahead came a **slurp** and a **grumble!**

Three minutes: a gurgling *burp!* Well, how rude . . .

it was **Belch,** loudly gobbling platefuls of food!

One thing was for certain:

Belch knew how to **eat!**

The dinosaurs **groaned**
and admitted defeat.

Two minutes to bed: but look!

Someone was swimming!

Rumble blinked his tired eyes.

It was Splash –
she was winning!

The **swift** little mermaid
swam up to meet Rumble.

Time for a final race

back to the jungle!

One minute: he yawned as he passed a big cave.
In the distance, he saw a **flag** starting to wave!

From the finishing line came a deafening roar –

who was the winner? It looked like a draw!

But wait – where was Rumble? Too tired to run . . .

he was curled up, asleep,
in the late evening sun.

THE·LAND·OF
NOD

THE
BLACK
MOUNTAIN

THE
FLOATING
ISLES

SNOWY
VILLAGE

ENCHANTED
VALLEY

CREEPY
CASTLE

GLOOMY
DEN

BOULDER
GORGE

GLITTER
BAY

N
W   E
S

THE
ANCIENT FOREST

OUTER
SPACE

EMERALD GLEN

DEADLY
CREEK

GIANTS' TOWN

THE
STINKY
SWAMPS

GOLDEN
COVE

RICKETY
BRIDGE

Look out for more bedtime adventures in THE·LAND·OF NOD

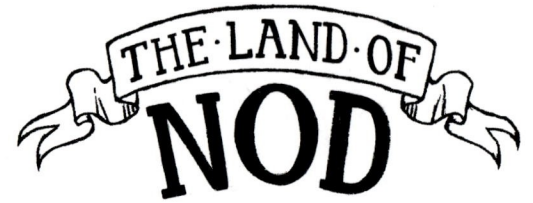

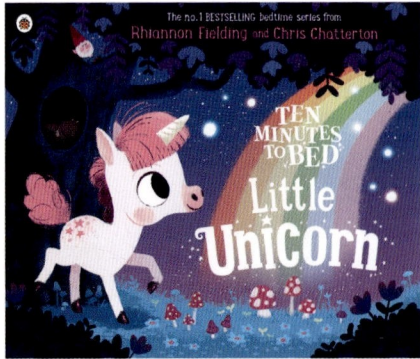

The no.1 BESTSELLING bedtime series from Rhiannon Fielding and Chris Chatterton
TEN MINUTES TO BED Little Unicorn

ISBN: 9780241348925

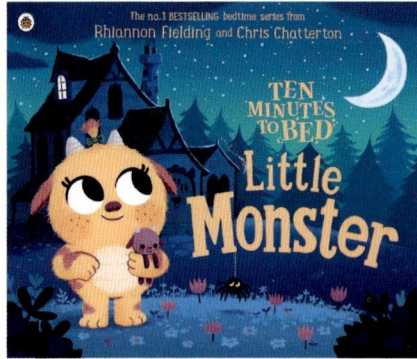

The no.1 BESTSELLING bedtime series from Rhiannon Fielding and Chris Chatterton
TEN MINUTES TO BED Little Monster

ISBN: 9780241348918

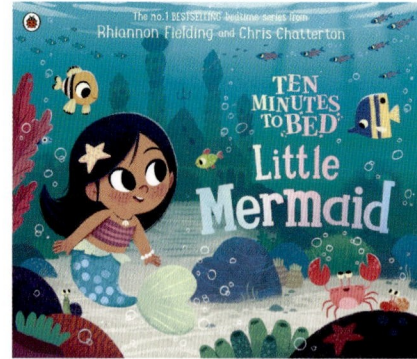

The no.1 BESTSELLING bedtime series from Rhiannon Fielding and Chris Chatterton
TEN MINUTES TO BED Little Mermaid

ISBN: 9780241372678

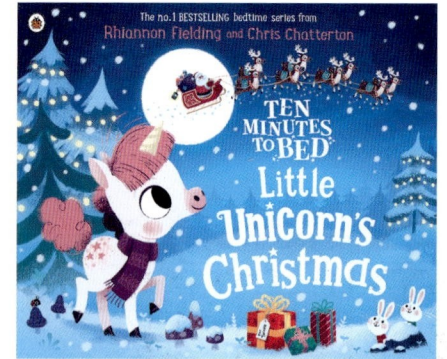

The no.1 BESTSELLING bedtime series from Rhiannon Fielding and Chris Chatterton
TEN MINUTES TO BED Little Unicorn's Christmas

ISBN: 9780241414576

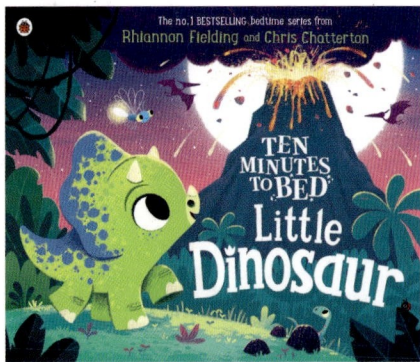

The no.1 BESTSELLING bedtime series from Rhiannon Fielding and Chris Chatterton
TEN MINUTES TO BED Little Dinosaur

ISBN: 9780241386736

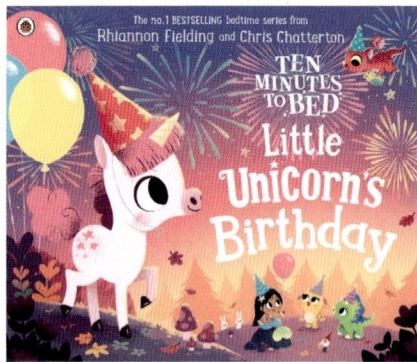

The no.1 BESTSELLING bedtime series from Rhiannon Fielding and Chris Chatterton
TEN MINUTES TO BED Little Unicorn's Birthday

ISBN: 9780241453162

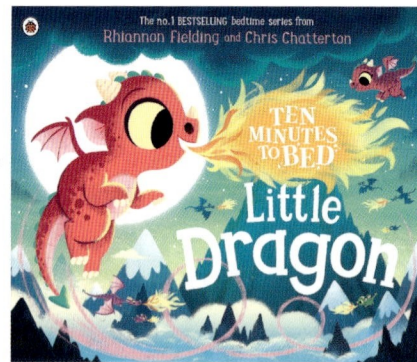

The no.1 BESTSELLING bedtime series from Rhiannon Fielding and Chris Chatterton
TEN MINUTES TO BED Little Dragon

ISBN: 9780241464373

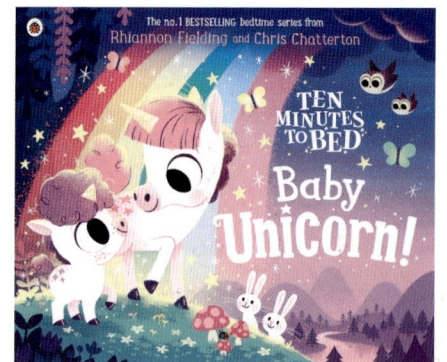

The no.1 BESTSELLING bedtime series from Rhiannon Fielding and Chris Chatterton
TEN MINUTES TO BED Baby Unicorn!

ISBN: 9780241464397

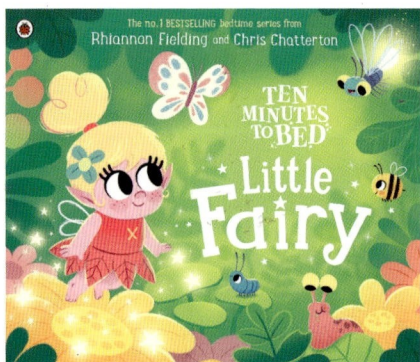

The no.1 BESTSELLING bedtime series from Rhiannon Fielding and Chris Chatterton
TEN MINUTES TO BED Little Fairy

ISBN: 9780241545591

The no.1 BESTSELLING bedtime series from Rhiannon Fielding and Chris Chatterton
TEN MINUTES TO BED Little Dinosaur's Big Race

ISBN: 9780241545638 ✓